Praise for

Mickey on the Move

"A HEARTWARMING AND UNFORGETTABLE STORY"

– Readers' Favorite

Purple Dragonfly Award
Recipient for Special Needs/Disability Awareness category

Named among the best in family-friendly media, products, and services by the **Mom's Choice Awards.**

Dedicated to my son, Charles Mikhail Wagner, who has shown me unconditional love and made this world a better place. To Mickey's dad, Charles Frank Wagner, who helps and supports Mickey every step of the way to give him the best possible life and gave him the tools to help make his education a success. And to Mickey's stepdad, Rick Lee Thompson, who has helped nurture and love Mickey in his adolescent years and worked with me to make my farming dreams come true.

www.mascotbooks.com

Mickey on the Move: Farming

For more information, please contact:
Mascot Books
620 Herndon Parkway, Suite 320
Herndon, VA 20170
info@mascotbooks.com

Library of Congress Control Number: 2021924433

CPSIA Code: PRT0122A

ISBN-13: 978-1-63755-242-1

Printed in the United States

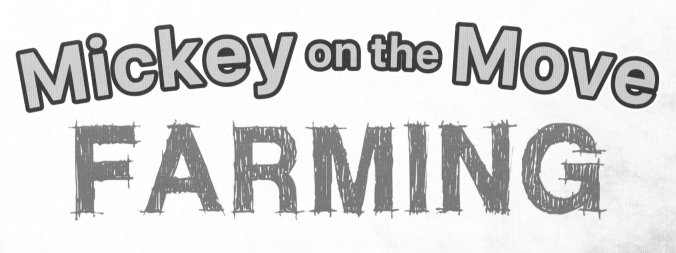

Mickey on the Move
FARMING

Michelle Wagner

Illustrated by Jenny Phelps

"**G**ood morning, chicks! Rise and shine!" Smiling ear to ear, Mickey called out to his chickens as he watched them prance down a ladder he made for their bright, red chicken coop.

Lately, "the early bird catches the worm" seemed to be the phrase that best described Mickey's eagerness when he got up every morning! Waking up to tend to his fluffy chickens after a night away was the best part of his day.

When Mickey is home with his mom, chickens aren't the only things they raise! The two of them have a garden, too, and Mickey loves eating all of the delicious fruits and vegetables.

Together, they grow herbs for seasoning the meals they make together, and their orchard is filled with everything from pears and plums to nectarines, figs, and even walnuts! There is always something new and tasty to discover.

More than anything else, Mickey loves
to be outside, moving around and
exploring. With a love of animals
and nature, he can always be
found running in the dirt
or splashing in a creek.

Since he was only two years old, Mickey would often be discovered between grapevines at his dad's vineyard, stuffing his little cheeks full of grapes with his shoes full of mud and a twinkle in his eye.

Mickey's dad is a fourth-generation Napa Valley grape grower and farmer, and Mickey loves to help make all kinds of things out of the grapes that are grown at the vineyard.

There were some obstacles early on in Mickey's life that he had to conquer in order to fully enjoy the great outdoors. Mickey doesn't hear things the same way that many kids do, and he uses cochlear implants, which allow him to listen to things he otherwise might not be able to hear—like quiet music or birds singing.

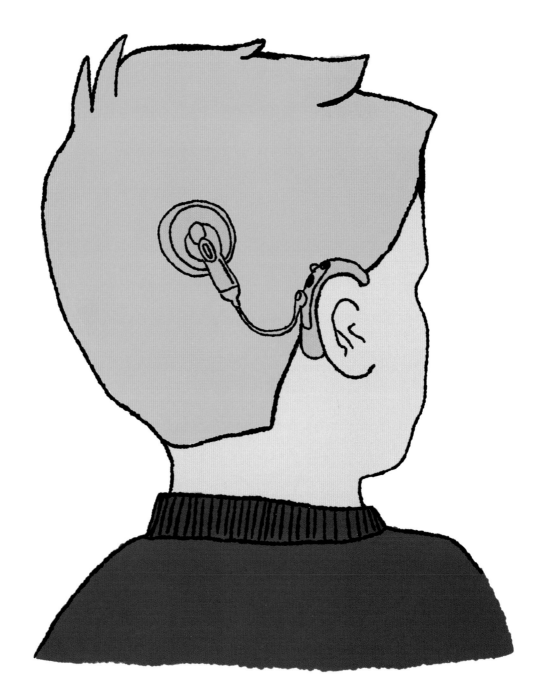

Cochlear implants are like tiny computers in your head—but just like how you can't get your own computer wet, Mickey couldn't get his implants wet!

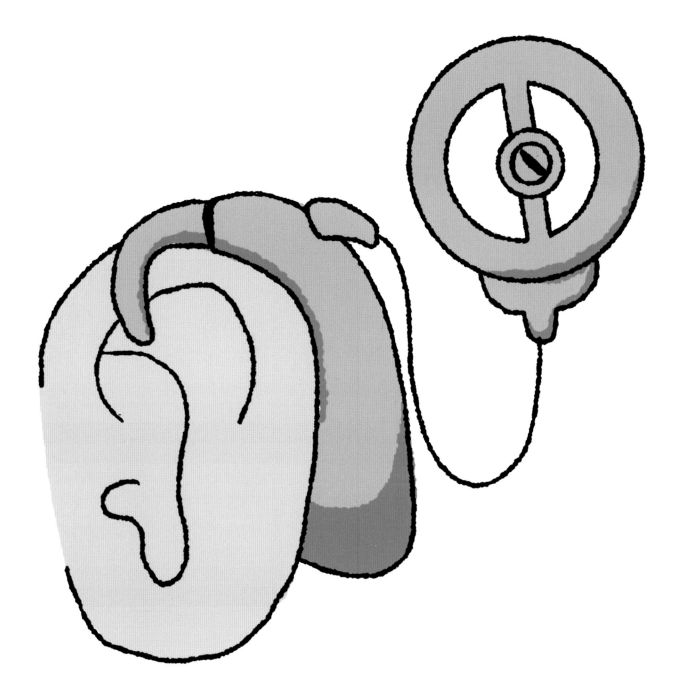

For example, if sprinklers turned on when Mickey was nearby, or if he splashed in a puddle too much, his cochlears would be ruined.

It didn't matter whether there was a sudden storm or he slipped into a pond—if water got on the implants, they would break, and Mickey wouldn't be able to hear at all.

uckily, an amazing organization called Cochlear Americas created the Aqua Cochlear, which means that Mickey can now swim, run in a sprinkler, or get wet when he wears them!

One day, when Mickey and his mom were picking carrots from their garden, the sky became overcast and it began to pour down rain! Normally, they would run inside to take shelter from the water, but this time . . .

. . . Mickey started jumping in a mud puddle! The rain came fast and hard, and he began to run through the garden, feeling the rain on his face. Mickey's mom joined him, and together they played until the sun came out!

 ow, Mickey loves the rain—especially the really loud storms! And when his dad accidentally sprays him with water when they're taking care of the vineyard and farm, Mickey laughs instead of covering his ears! Giving his chickens something to drink has never been easier, too!

With his Aqua Cochlear, a whole new world of possibilities opens up for Mickey, and he and his mom are determined to try every new thing they can find!

The End!

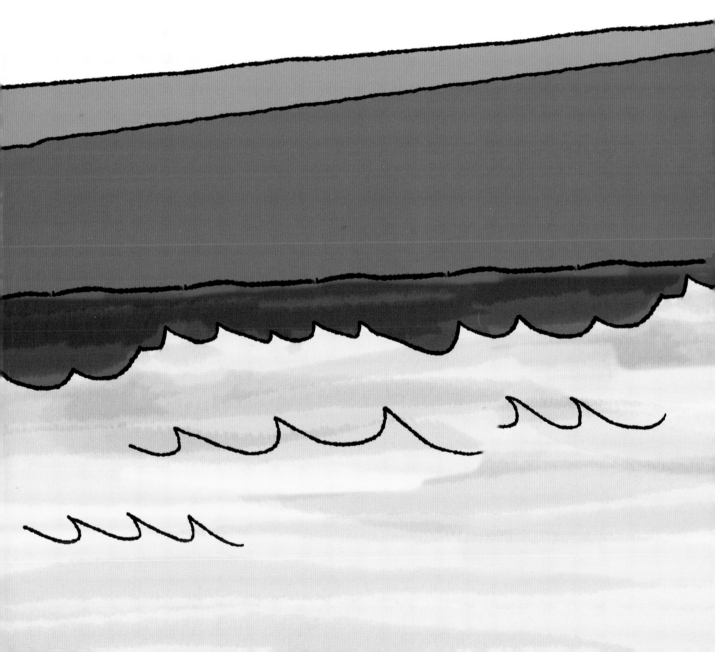

About the Author

Michelle Wagner is a full-time realtor, mom, and award-winning author who dedicates her time and energy to charities and events supporting children with hearing loss. Michelle takes pride in assisting families as they work through the different approaches to raising a special-needs child in a typical environment.

After discovering that her son Mickey was profoundly deaf in both ears, Michelle made it her mission to provide Mickey with the tools to ensure that he would live his best life. Today, Mickey, who wears bilateral cochlear implants, plays tennis and is currently in eighth grade at the St. Helena Montessori Farm School, where he is thriving and is social with his friends. Michelle makes sure that Mickey has the courage to be his optimal self.